Tony Bradman

DILLY
AND THE GHOST

Stories of the World's Naughtiest Dinosaur

Illustrated by Susan Hellard

MAMMOTH

First published 1989 by Piccadilly Press Ltd
Published 1990 by Mammoth
an imprint of Mandarin paperbacks
Michelin House, 81 Fulham Road, London SW3 6RB

Mandarin is an imprint of the Octopus Publishing Group

Text copyright © Tony Bradman, 1989
Illustrations copyright © Susan Hellard, 1989

ISBN 0 7497 0247 8

A CIP catalogue record for this title
is available from the British Library

Printed in Great Britain
by Cox & Wyman Ltd, Reading

DILLY GOES TO THE BEACH

At breakfast yesterday morning, Mother and Father gave us a wonderful surprise.

'How would you two like to go to the beach today?' Father said.

Dilly looked at me, and I looked at Dilly. And we both said . . .

'Hooray!'

I was glad, but Dilly was *really* pleased. If there's one thing he enjoys almost more than anything else, it's a trip to the beach. He started jumping up and down with excitement.

'Can we go now?' he said. 'Now! Now! Now!'

'Whoa there, Dilly,' said Father, 'will you calm down a little? You look as if someone's set your tail on fire. We won't be going anywhere if you behave like that.'

Dilly stopped jumping up and down. I could see he wanted to go to the beach very much.

'That's better,' said Father. 'We all want to enjoy our day at the beach, which means we don't want it spoiled by a naughty little dinosaur. So do you promise you'll be good today?'

'Yes, Father,' said Dilly, with his really-I'm-the-nicest-little-dinosaur-in-the-world-look on his face. 'I promise.'

'Just try your best, anyway,' said Father.

Dilly said he would.

Father made a picnic lunch while Mother, Dilly and I loaded the dino-car. Dilly was very helpful. He seemed determined to prove he could be well behaved. It didn't take long to get to the beach, and when we arrived, we were pleased to see it wasn't crowded.

'Doesn't it look lovely?' said Mother. She was right. Dinosaurs love lying in the sun and splashing in water almost as much as they love mud wallowing, and the beach is perfect for all those things. It's a long curve of fine, golden sand round the bay where the water's always clean and clear. Behind the dunes there

are some giant palm trees, with mud
pools nearby.

We found some big, flat rocks to bask
on, and Mother put up the parasol so we
could have some shade. Father and I
unloaded the dino-car. Dilly helped too.

'Come here now, Dilly and Dorla,'
said Mother when we'd finished. 'You've
got to have some sun cream on.'

I don't mind sun cream. Mother says it
stops the sun burning you, and helps
your skin turn a lovely dark green
colour. Dilly really hates it, though. He

4

says it makes him feel slimy, and the sand sticks to him. So usually he shouts and screams and says he won't have any on. But today he didn't.

'OK, Mother,' he said, and went over to her obediently.

Mother and Father did some basking and reading, and Dilly didn't pester them once. Father went swimming, and tried out a new tail flipper he'd bought. We built a huge sand-castle, with a moat full of water we fetched from the sea in our buckets. Then we collected some shells and seaweed.

The morning went by very quickly. After lunch, we bought ice creams from the little shop at the other end of the beach. Dilly wanted a Frozen Pineapple Delight, but they didn't have any. He didn't complain, even though he loves pineapple juice, and settled for a fern-flavoured Tail Tingler instead.

'I'm very pleased with you today, Dilly,' said Father, as we walked back along the beach. 'You *are* keeping your promise.'

Dilly just smiled. I could hardly

believe it – for once, he was being a real goody two-shoes. A little later, I heard Mother say she thought Dilly was being good because he was enjoying himself so much. Father agreed, and said they shouldn't let him get bored.

So I wasn't surprised when Father asked us to play Find The Treasure. We said yes straight away – it's our favourite beach game. We each get a turn to bury something in the sand, while everyone else keeps their eyes covered, so they don't know what you've chosen or where it is. Then they have to find it.

It was Father's turn first. He buried the tube of sun cream near the rocks, but he'd left so many paw prints in the sand nearby we knew where to start looking as soon as we opened our eyes.

'You're cold,' said Father, laughing. 'Cold . . . warm, warmer — now you're

7

hot, very hot! You've found it! You must have been cheating! But I'll let you off this time . . . your turn next, Dorla.'

It was lots of fun. We played for ages, right up until it was time to go home.

'Come on, everybody,' said Father at last. 'We'd better start packing everything up.'

'Can I have another turn, Father?' said Dilly. 'Just one more, please?'

'OK, Dilly,' said Father, 'seeing as you've been such a good little dinosaur today. But it will have to be a quick turn. It's getting late.'

We all covered our eyes while Dilly went off to bury something. He called out when he'd finished, and we started looking. We searched, and we searched, but we couldn't find anything. Dilly kept telling us how cold we were. We didn't get warm, not even *once*. Finally Father stopped playing and looked at his watch.

'I'd better start loading some things in the car while you play,' he said. He reached into his pocket. Then he reached into his other pocket. Soon he was looking in all his pockets, and all the bags.

'I can't find the keys to the dino-car,' he said at last. 'I wonder where they can be?' Then he looked at Dilly. 'You haven't buried them, have you, Dilly?'

'No, Father,' said Dilly.

'Are you sure, Dilly? We can't go home without them.'

Dilly said he was sure, but I don't think Father believed him.

'Now, Dilly,' he said, 'you promised to be good today. A game's a game, but we need those keys. Where have you buried them?'

'But I *haven't* buried them, Father,' said Dilly. He was beginning to look a little upset.

Father looked really cross. In fact, his face went dark green, and he started to shout so loudly that most of the other

dinosaurs on the beach turned to look at us.

'You will tell me where you've buried the keys *this instant*!' he shouted. He even stamped his foot like Dilly does when he's having a tantrum.

'Actually, dear, I think . . . ' Mother started to say.

'Not now,' Father snapped. 'Well, Dilly? You're going to be in a lot of trouble unless you tell me. I'm waiting.'

Mother tried again. 'But dear, I really think you ought . . . '

'Not *now*!' Father shouted at her. 'Right, Dilly,' said Father. 'I'll count to three . . . '

Father never even made it to one. Dilly opened his mouth and let rip with an ultra-special, 150-mile-per-hour super-scream. We all dived for cover, and the beach emptied in seconds.

He calmed down in the end, and so
did Father. Dilly had only buried one of
the shells we'd found, and Mother had
been trying to tell Father she thought
he'd left the keys in his jacket. It was
lying near the rock he'd been basking
on. He felt in the pockets . . . and there
they were.

Father was very embarrassed, and
didn't say much on the way home.

Later, at bedtime, I heard him go into
Dilly's room and apologise.

'I'm sorry, Dilly,' he said. 'You did
keep your promise today, after all. And

you were so good, we've decided to take you and Dorla back to the beach tomorrow. What do you think of that?'

Dilly was quiet for a moment.

'We all want to enjoy our day at the beach, Father,' he said at last. I could hear he was imitating Father's voice! 'That means we don't want it spoiled by you losing your temper again. So do you promise you'll be good?'

'Yes, Dilly,' said Father. 'I promise.'

'Well, just try your best,' said Dilly.

And then they both laughed!

DILLY AND THE LOOSE TOOTH

A few weeks ago one of my teeth came out. It had been loose for ages, and I put it under my pillow before I went to sleep, the way Mother told me to. In the morning it had gone, and there was a bright, shiny coin in its place.

'Look, Mother,' I said at breakfast. 'The Tooth Pterodactyl took my tooth last night, and left me some money.'

'That's nice, Dorla,' said Mother.

'Let me see,' said Dilly. I showed him

the gap where my tooth had been, and the coin. 'But why did your tooth fall out?'

'Don't you know anything, silly Dilly?' I said. 'It's to let my new teeth grow through.'

'Now, now, Dorla,' said Mother. 'That's enough of that. Dilly doesn't understand about teeth coming out because it hasn't happened to him yet. It's quite simple, Dilly . . . '

Mother explained to Dilly all about teeth. She said that baby dinosaurs didn't have any when they hatched from their eggs, but soon grew some. When you were older, these baby teeth got loose and fell out. They were replaced by bigger, stronger teeth, the sort you would need to chew fern stalks with when you were a grown-up dinosaur.

'So when will *my* teeth fall out?'

'I don't know, Dilly,' said Mother. 'I suppose Dorla was a little older than you when she had her first loose tooth. But you might have to wait a bit longer.'

'But that's not fair,' said Dilly. He was beginning to look very grumpy. 'I want one of my teeth to come out, and I want the Tooth Pterodactyl to bring me some money . . . *now*!' Dilly stamped his foot – STAMP! STAMP!

'Now, Dilly,' said Mother. 'The Tooth Pterodactyl only visits good little dinosaurs, the sort who clean their teeth regularly. She doesn't visit little dinosaurs who shout and stamp their feet. So you'll have to be on your best behaviour, won't you?'

Dilly stopped stamping.

'I will be, Mother,' he said, smiling and showing all his teeth.

He was well-behaved for a while, too. He didn't do any of the naughty things he usually does – but he did keep talking about loose teeth and the Tooth Pterodactyl. In fact, hardly a moment went by without Dilly pestering Mother about them. Every time she helped him brush his teeth, he made her check *each one* to see if any were wobbly.

One day Mother got quite cross about it. It was Hallowe'en, and Mother and Father had said I could have a fancy dress party for my friends. I was really excited. But there was lots to do, and Mother was very busy.

'Mother,' said Dilly while she was decorating the table for the party, 'I think one of my teeth is coming out.'

Mother didn't even stop what she was doing to look in Dilly's mouth.

'I'm sure it isn't, Dilly,' she said. 'If I've told you once, I've told you a thousand times, you'll just have to be a little more patient.'

'But, Mother,' said Dilly, 'I want a tooth for the Tooth Pterodactyl.'

'If I could find one to give you, Dilly,' said Mother, 'I would. But I can't at the moment . . . now where did I put those paper plates?'

Dilly looked surprised.

'Does the Tooth Pterodactyl take *any* teeth?' he said. 'And does he give you money for them?'

'What, Dilly?' said Mother. 'I suppose so . . . now will you run along and play?

I've got to get those swamp worm cakes
into the cooker or they'll never be
ready.'

Mother went into the kitchen, and
Dilly stood there for a while with his
thoughtful look on his face. I couldn't
wait around worrying about Dilly,
though. I had to get on and help
Mother.

We finally had everything ready just
before my friends were due to arrive.
Father had carved a giant swamp
mushroom to look like a face and fitted a
candle inside it. We put it in the window
and it looked really spooky.

Mother had made lots of special Hallowe'en food, too. There was a big bowl of steaming marsh-water soup, just like a witch's cauldron, swamp potatoes baked in their jackets, and candied fern stalks in the shape of bat wings.

I still had to get into my witch's costume. Father had helped me make it. There was a big, black pointy hat, a ragged dress, a huge cloak, and a

broomstick to ride on. Mother helped me make up with face paints – we even made some warts out of plasticine. Father said he was scared to look at me!

But I wasn't as scary as some of my friends. Lots of them came dressed as witches, of course, and most of the costumes were terrific. But when Doni arrived, everyone screamed and ran away because he was so terrifying. He was dressed as a . . . *human being*.

My best friend Deena came as Count Dinula, the vampire. She had a black cloak and a bow tie, but best of all, she had these amazing vampire teeth. She had bought them at a joke shop in the Shopping Cavern, and they were so good they looked real.

Dilly couldn't take his eyes off them.

'Your teeth look very sharp, Deena,' he said.

'Urrmmf er, urrmmff . . . ' Deena couldn't speak properly while the teeth were in her mouth. She took them out. 'Don't worry, Dilly,' she said. 'I won't bite you.'

Deena put the teeth down on the table next to her plate. Dilly was sitting next to her, and I could see him staring at them. He looked absolutely fascinated.

I was worried that Dilly would be naughty. He usually is when I have a party, but this time he wasn't. Mother had made him a costume – he was dressed as a little demon. He joined in

all our games, except when we were
Trick or Treating. Mother and Father
said he was too young, even though we
were only going to the houses nearby
with Father.

'You can stay here instead and help
me tidy up, Dilly,' said Mother. I
wondered whether he would make a fuss
– but he didn't. In fact, oddly enough,
he looked really pleased.

Soon it was time for everyone to go
home. It had been a wonderful party.
The only problem was that Deena
couldn't find her vampire teeth. They'd

disappeared. Mother said they would probably turn up in the morning, and that Deena wasn't to worry.

'Come on, Dilly,' said Father when the last guest had gone, 'it's time you were in bed.'

Now usually after he's been doing something exciting, Dilly won't go to bed. But tonight he didn't say a word. In fact he practically *ran* upstairs. Father was really surprised.

'Dilly's acting very strangely tonight,' he said to Mother when he came downstairs. 'He got straight into bed, lay down with his arms by his sides, closed his eyes and said good night. He didn't even want any stories.'

Mother said she thought he was probably very tired after the party, and we thought no more about it. Soon it was time for me to go to bed, and I went straight to sleep too.

The next morning, I hadn't been awake very long when I heard Dilly jump out of bed. He was quiet for a second . . . and then he let rip with an ultra-special, 150-mile-per-hour super-scream, the sort that makes everyone come running to see what's wrong.

Dilly was standing by his bed. The pillow was on the floor, and where it should have been we could all see . . .

Deena's vampire teeth! Dilly must have taken them the night before, and put them under his pillow for the Tooth Pterodactyl.

But she hadn't come for them. Dilly had screamed when he had looked under his pillow and found the teeth still there – and no bright, shiny coin.

Of course, Mother gave Dilly quite a telling off for being deceitful and taking something that didn't belong to him. Dilly said he was sorry, and Mother said she hoped he had learned his lesson.

'The Tooth Pterodactyl will only give you money for your *own* teeth,' I heard her saying later when she was helping Dilly brush his teeth. 'And I don't think you'll have to wait much longer, now, Dilly. I do believe this tooth in the front is a little wobbly. Are you pleased?'

'Yes, Mother,' he said. And he did sound very pleased indeed.

'So am I, Dilly,' said Mother. 'So am I.'

DILLY AND THE X-RAY

Dilly loves riding around on his little dino-trike. He can go really fast on it, too. The trouble is that sometimes he doesn't look where he's going.

Take yesterday, for instance. We were playing in the garden. Dilly was pretending he was Super Dinosaur, and that his dino-trike was rocket powered like one he'd seen in a programme on TV.

'Broomm, broomm!' he shouted.

'You're the evil villain, and I'm coming to get you, Dorla!'

Then he put his head down and pedalled as fast as he could towards me. I got out of the way, but Dilly didn't notice. He shot past and crashed into the giant fern. He flew over the handlebars, bounced off the trunk and lay there on the grass.

Mother and I ran up to him. He was a very pale green, and there was a big bump on his forehead. It seemed to get bigger and bigger before our eyes.

'Are you all right, Dilly?' Mother said. I could see she was very worried.

At first Dilly didn't say anything. But he did open his eyes after a while, and then he started to cry. Mother picked him up and carried him into the house. She put him down on the sofa and had another look at the bump on his head.

Father looked at it too.

Then Mother and Father whispered together. Dilly was beginning to look a little better now. He wasn't quite so pale, and he'd stopped crying. But the bump was very big and had gone a nasty yellow colour.

'My head hurts, Mother,' said Dilly at last.

'I'm not surprised,' said Mother. 'That's quite some bump you've got there . . . I think we ought to take you to the hospital to get it looked at.'

Dilly didn't seem to be worried about going to the hospital. I think that's because one of his favourite games is playing doctors. We've got a toy doctor's outfit, and Dilly really enjoys pretending to be a patient. He especially likes being covered in bandages.

'Will they give me a bandage for my head at the hospital, Mother?' he said when we were in the dino-car on our way there.

'I should think so, Dilly,' said Mother. Dilly smiled for the first time since his accident.

The hospital is very big, with lots of different parts. When we arrived we didn't know where to go. Mother and Father stood in front of a big board covered in signs with arrows pointing in every direction.

'Administration . . . surgery . . . ah, here it is,' said Father. 'Accident and emergency.'

We started walking towards some
doors. Lots of other dinosaurs were
going that way, too. We went into a
large room and up to a desk, where a
nice dinosaur nurse wrote down Dilly's
name and what had happened to him.
She said we would have to wait, so we
found some seats and sat down.

Dilly seemed a lot better now. The
bump was just as big and yellow, but the
rest of his face had got its proper green

colour back. He was looking round at all the other dinosaurs, and he was full of questions, too.

'Father, what does admin . . . admin . . . what does that word mean, and the other one you said?'

Father explained both words. He said that administration was another word for the offices where the people who ran the hospital worked.

'And surgery means having an operation,' he said. 'That's when the doctor has to cut someone open to look in their insides and make them better.'

Dilly looked very thoughtful for a second. He was about to ask another question when he saw something that made him stop and stare.

'Why is that grown-up dinosaur being pushed like a baby, Mother?' he said in a loud voice. He was pointing at an old

dinosaur in a wheelchair. Mother looked very embarrassed.

'I don't know how many times I've told you it's rude to point, Dilly. And keep your voice down,' Mother hissed. She explained that the old dinosaur was probably too ill to walk, so he had to ride in a wheelchair to see the doctor.

'Mother,' he said, 'can I have a ride in a wheelchair? My head still hurts a lot.'

'I think you'll be able to walk when it's your turn to see the doctor, Dilly,' said Mother.

And she was right. There was nothing wrong with Dilly's legs. Soon he was running round the waiting room, staring at all the other dinosaurs and talking to them, climbing on the chairs and pestering the nurse at the desk. Mother told him off and tried to make him sit still. But nobody seemed to mind that much.

We had to wait a long time, but the nurse called out Dilly's name at last. We had to go through a door into a small room. A doctor in a white coat was waiting for us.

She was very nice. She said hello to Dilly, and looked at his bump. She said

35

she thought it was the biggest bump on the head she'd ever seen. Dilly smiled.

'I think a bump like that calls for an X-ray,' said the doctor. She wrote something on a piece of paper, and said we had to go to another part of the hospital. So off we went.

'Father, what's an X-ray?' said Dilly.

'It's a little difficult to explain, Dilly,' said Father. 'Ah . . . here we are. You'll soon find out.'

We went into another room. But this one was full of huge pieces of machinery and a great big table.

'Right, Dilly,' said the doctor. 'Up on the table . . . we're just going to have a look inside your head to make sure everything is all right.'

Dilly shrank back against Mother.

'Come along, Dilly,' said the doctor. 'There's nothing to be worried about.'

Dilly didn't say anything.

'It's OK, Dilly,' said Mother. 'It will be over very quickly.'

I don't think Dilly believed her. He looked at the doctor in the white coat, who stood there smiling.

Then Dilly opened his mouth and . . . that's right, you guessed it, he let rip with a 150-mile-per hour, ultra-special super-scream, the kind that makes doctors jump into cupboards, and shatters the glass test tubes on a table in the corner.

It took ages to calm Dilly down. It
turned out that when the doctor said he
was going to have a look inside his head,
Dilly had thought it meant he was going
to have an operation.

'Oh no,' said the doctor, laughing.
'I've got a magic camera that can take
pictures of what's inside your head,
that's all.'

Dilly was beginning to look quite
interested. The doctor showed him other
dinosaurs' X-rays.

'So you see, Dilly,' said the doctor,
'we can tell all sorts of things with X-rays.
So will you let me take your X-ray now?'

Dilly was quiet for a moment.

'OK,' he said, 'I'll let you do it. But
only if you let me have something . . . '
Dilly whispered in the doctor's ear.

Dilly's X-ray was fine. As the doctor
said, there wasn't much wrong with him

at all. He got his bandage, even though he didn't really need one. And he also got the other thing he wanted . . . a ride in a wheelchair!

Mother pushed him in one from the X-ray room all the way to the dino-car.

'Mother,' said Dilly when we got home, 'about my X-ray.'

'Yes, Dilly?' said Mother. 'What about it?'

'Well, when the doctor takes a picture of what's inside my head, does that mean he can tell what I'm thinking, too?'

'No, Dilly,' Mother laughed. 'That's something *nobody* will ever be able to do!'

DILLY AND THE GHOST

'Right, Dilly,' said Father one evening at bedtime, 'what stories would you like tonight? How about *Hey Diddle Dinosaur*? It looks really good.'

'I don't want that one,' said Dilly making a face. 'It's silly. Can I have this, instead?' He reached under his pillow and handed Father a book.

'What's this?' said Father. '*The Ghost of Fern Tree Forest*? It might be a little scary, Dilly. It's one of Dorla's, isn't it?'

It was, too. Dilly is always coming into my room and taking my books. He can't read them, but he likes looking at the pictures. And ever since my Hallowe'en party, he especially wants books about witches and ghosts.

'But I *like* scary stories,' he said. 'And I want you to read it to me.'

'Well . . . ' said Father, 'I don't know, Dilly . . . '

'Please, Father,' he said. '*Please.*'

'OK, Dilly,' said Father. 'But you're to stop me the moment it gets too scary for you. I don't want you having nightmares.'

So Father started reading *The Ghost of Fern Tree Forest*. It's about a family of dinosaurs who discover their house is haunted. The doors creak and open by themselves, and something howls in the middle of the night . . .

'Well, that's quite enough of *that* for one evening,' said Father when he got to the end of the first chapter. 'I think you're a little young for this sort of thing, Dilly.'

'I'm not,' said Dilly. 'I think it's *fantastic*.' I could see he was telling the truth. Usually at story time Dilly climbs all over Father and bounces up and down on the bed. But Dilly had sat perfectly still during the story, wide-eyed and listening.

He didn't have any nightmares, either. He made Father read *The Ghost of Fern Tree Forest* all the way through over the next couple of weeks. He talked about ghosts and the story all the time.

'I liked the part where the ghost came down the stairs,' he said one morning at breakfast. 'Do you remember, Father? It was really scary.'

'I certainly do, Dilly,' said Father. 'By the way, I thought we might go to the library later today to get some new books for bedtime.'

Dilly smiled.

'Can I get a new ghost book, Father?' he said. 'Please?'

'I suppose so, Dilly,' said Father with a sigh. I could see he didn't look very happy. Mother smiled.

'What's the matter, dear?' she said. 'I don't think your father likes ghost stories very much, Dilly. Perhaps they're a little too scary for *him*.'

We all laughed, and I saw Mother wink at Father. I don't think Dilly did, though. He was too busy giving Father a funny look.

Dilly got a pile of ghost books from the library, and Father read him all of them. Dilly thought they were terrific.

Then one night, a very strange thing happened.

We were all sitting watching TV, when suddenly there was a creaking noise . . . *creeeeeakkkk* . . . and the sitting room door opened all by itself.

'Now that's odd,' said Father. He stood up, looked round the door into the hall, and shut it.

Mother said it was probably a draught from an open window. But none of the windows were open.

'I know what it was,' said Dilly. Everyone looked at him. 'We've got a . . . GHOST!'

'Don't be silly, Dilly,' said Father. 'There's no such thing.'

Dilly didn't say anything. But when Father wasn't looking, I could see him smiling secretly to himself. I began to realise that Dilly was up to something.

You could almost see his little mind working . . .

At bedtime that evening, Father started reading a new ghost story about a haunted cave to Dilly. I could hear his voice from my bedroom.

'And just then,' he was saying, 'there was a noise . . . '

'Ssshh, Father,' Dilly said.

'What, Dilly?' said Father. 'What is it?'

'Ssshh . . . ' said Dilly. 'I can hear something.'

'What can you hear?' said Father. I thought he sounded a little . . . worried.

'I don't know,' said Dilly. 'It's a sort of whistling, or someone going "Whooooo " . . . '

Father went quiet for a moment.

'Oh, this is ridiculous,' he said after a while. 'I suppose you'll be telling me next it's a ghost.'

46

'It isn't *a* ghost, Father,' said Dilly.

'I'm glad to hear you say so, Dilly,' said Father.

'No . . . it's *our* ghost. The one that lives with us.'

Father got quite cross then, and said he wouldn't read any more of the ghost story if Dilly was going to misbehave. So Dilly said he was sorry, and Father kept reading.

Later, after I heard Father say good night and go downstairs, I sneaked into Dilly's room. I knew he must be up to something.

At first he wouldn't tell me. Then he said he really *did* believe we had a ghost, and he was just trying to make Father believe it too. But nothing he did seemed to work.

'It would help if Father actually saw a ghost,' I said. 'So . . . why don't *you* pretend to be one?'

I'd read a story once about someone who pretended to be a ghost. All he'd done was to put a sheet over his head and make lots of moaning noises, like the ghosts you see in TV programmes. Dilly said that was what he was planning anyway. Then he would walk down the stairs like the ghost in *The Ghost of Fern Tree Forest*.

We both thought it was a really terrific idea. Dilly jumped out of bed and pulled a sheet off right then and there. I said I'd go back to my room and wait until I heard him on the landing.

I got into bed and waited. Nothing happened for a while, although I did hear some strange noises coming from Dilly's room. I was just about to go and see what he was doing, when Dilly's bedroom door opened and the landing light clicked off.

There was a swishing noise, and a pale shape appeared in the dark at the top of the stairs. It made a really scary noise – *whoooooo . . .* , it went. *Whoooooo . . .*

Even though I knew it was only Dilly
pretending to be a ghost, it made me feel
shivery all over.

'Is that you, Dilly? What's happened
to the light?' It was Father's voice. Dilly
didn't answer. He just kept moaning and
swishing down the stairs.

I peeked round my door, and just at
that moment, Father turned on the light.
He was right in front of Dilly, with a
strange look on his face. He even
seemed a little . . . scared. But when he
saw what Dilly had done to his sheet, he
wasn't frightened – he was very, very
cross.

Dilly had cut two holes in the sheet for
his eyes, and drawn all over it with his
crayons. So that was what he'd been
doing in his room! Father said it was
completely ruined, and that Dilly was
the naughtiest dinosaur there had ever

been. I said it had been my idea to use the sheet, so I got told off too.

By now, Dilly was getting upset, and when Father said he couldn't go to Dixie's the next day to play, you can guess what happened. That's right, he let rip with a 150-mile-per-hour, ultra-special super-scream, the kind that would frighten any ghost out of its wits. At least that's what Father said.

The next morning, Dilly said he was sorry.

'Well, Dilly,' said Mother, 'you were very naughty. You've ruined that sheet . . . but it *was* almost worth it to see the look on your Father's face.'

'You weren't really frightened, were you, Father?' said Dilly.

'No, of course not,' said Father.

'So will you read me a ghost story tonight?'

'Er . . . ' Father began to say. But Mother didn't give him a chance to finish.

'Of course he will, Dilly. He loves ghosts,' she said. And we all laughed – even Father!

DILLY, THE WORST DAY EVER

Dilly is the *naughtiest* dinosaur in the whole world and he has a 150 mph scream!

This is another collection of Dilly adventures and Dilly is trying to turn over a new leaf. But everything goes wrong! The harder he tries, the worse things get . . .

DILLY AND THE HORROR FILM

The naughtiest dinosaur in the world is staying with granny for the evening. It's movie time! They both get a fright when the late film turns out to be a spooky one. Having a 150 mph scream can have its problems . . .

DILLY TELLS THE TRUTH

Dilly always tries to be good and tell the truth but he's only human – and things are bound to go wrong! Dilly the naughty little dinosaur is growing up funnier than ever!

MEET THE WORLD'S NAUGHTIEST DINOSAUR!

Even though, as everyone knows, he's the world's naughtiest dinosaur Dilly still has lots of fans. Now that he is so famous he's started making special visits to bookshops to meet the people who enjoy reading about him. You might be able to meet him in your local bookshop – he usually tries to behave himself!

If you would like to meet Dilly yourself ask your teacher or your librarian to invite him to visit your school or library. The address to write to is written below. You can also write to this address for more information about Dilly and his books and about other books published by MAMMOTH.

MAMMOTH Press Office,
38 Hans Crescent,
London SW1X 0LZ

A Selected List of Fiction from Mammoth

While every effort is made to keep prices low, it is sometimes necessary to increase prices at short notice. Mammoth Books reserves the right to show new retail prices on covers which may differ from those previously advertised in the text or elsewhere.

The prices shown below were correct at the time of going to press.

☐	7497 0366 0	**Dilly the Dinosaur**	Tony Bradman	£1.99
☐	7497 0021 1	**Dilly and the Tiger**	Tony Bradman	£1.99
☐	7497 0137 4	**Flat Stanley**	Jeff Brown	£1.99
☐	7497 0048 3	**Friends and Brothers**	Dick King-Smith	£1.99
☐	7497 0054 8	**My Naughty Little Sister**	Dorothy Edwards	£1.99
☐	416 86550 X	**Cat Who Wanted to go Home**	Jill Tomlinson	£1.99
☐	7497 0166 8	**The Witch's Big Toe**	Ralph Wright	£1.99
☐	7497 0218 4	**Lucy Jane at the Ballet**	Susan Hampshire	£2.25
☐	416 03212 5	**I Don't Want To!**	Bel Mooney	£1.99
☐	7497 0030 0	**I Can't Find It!**	Bel Mooney	£1.99
☐	7497 0032 7	**The Bear Who Stood on His Head**	W. J. Corbett	£1.99
☐	416 10362 6	**Owl and Billy**	Martin Waddell	£1.75
☐	416 13822 5	**It's Abigail Again**	Moira Miller	£1.75
☐	7497 0031 9	**King Tubbitum and the Little Cook**	Margaret Ryan	£1.99
☐	7497 0041 6	**The Quiet Pirate**	Andrew Matthews	£1.99
☐	7497 0064 5	**Grump and the Hairy Mammoth**	Derek Sampson	£1.99

All these books are available at your bookshop or newsagent, or can be ordered direct from the publisher. Just tick the titles you want and fill in the form below.

Mandarin Paperbacks, Cash Sales Department, PO Box 11, Falmouth, Cornwall TR10 9EN.

Please send cheque or postal order, no currency, for purchase price quoted and allow the following for postage and packing:

UK	80p for the first book, 20p for each additional book ordered to a maximum charge of £2.00.
BFPO	80p for the first book, 20p for each additional book.
Overseas including Eire	£1.50 for the first book, £1.00 for the second and 30p for each additional book thereafter.

NAME (Block letters) ....

ADDRESS ....

....

....